Charming Tales

for Little Girls

Thumbelina Tales
Written by Peter Holeinone
Illustrated by M.G. Boldorini

The Six Sisters Tales
Written and Illustrated by Rose Selarose

Adapations by Louise Gikow

★ A Tell-Me-A-Story Keepsake Treasury ★

Charming Tales
for Little Girls

Dalmatian
Press

CHARMING TALES *for* LITTLE GIRLS
Copyright © 2004 Dami International, Milano

Cover Design: Emily Robertson

Published in 2004 by Dalmatian Press, LLC.
The DALMATIAN PRESS name and logo are trademarks
of Dalmatian Press, LLC, Franklin, Tennessee 37067.

ISBN: 1-40370-769-3
13341-0504

04 05 06 07 SFO 10 9 8 7 6 5 4 3 2 1

Tell Me A Story.

When you read a story to your child, lots of good things happen. You show your child that reading is exciting and fun. You encourage the growth and development not just of your little one's imagination but also his or her vocabulary, comprehension skills, and overall school readiness.

Research shows, time and time again, that children who are read to on a regular basis do significantly better in school than children who are not read to at home. We encourage you to spend ten to twenty minutes every day reading to your child. It's a small amount of quality time that reaps a big reward!

It's also important to keep reading books *to* your child and *with* your child even after he or she is reading independently. You can share books that are slightly more difficult than what your child is reading on his or her own because you are available to help with vocabulary words and any questions your child may have about the story.

Read and Discuss.

No matter how old your child is, or how well she is reading independently, remember that story time is the perfect opportunity to talk about what you're reading and any other topics that might arise from it. This kind of dialog helps make stories come alive and adds depth to your child's reading experience.

What would you do if you were in the story? you might ask. *How might you fix this problem? Did the character do the right thing?* and so forth.

Your child's Keepsake Treasury includes dialogic questions throughout the stories to prompt meaningful and memorable conversations. Ask your own questions as well. You might be surprised at the imaginative discussions that follow. You can learn more about dialogic reading online at: *http://www.readingrockets.org.*

We hope that *Charming Tales for Little Girls* will become a treasured part of your family's library.

Happy Reading!

CONTENTS

THUMBELINA AND THE STAR

Thumbelina was a tiny girl, as tiny as a wee mouse. She was the daughter of two wicked giants.

The giants wanted giant children, but they got Thumbelina instead. This was because they had been very bad giants indeed.

And they were very bad to Thumbelina.

Thumbelina was so small that she could easily fit into a nutshell. And that's where her mother and father put her. Then they threw her into the river.

Poor Thumbelina!

Luckily for her, the current carried the nutshell into a tranquil pond. There, Thumbelina reached the bank and set off to find some friends.

"Ribbet! Ribbet!" called a big, green frog. "Get onto my back and I'll take you to the flowers!"

Thumbelina jumped on. She soon found herself in a meadow full of daisies.

"How do you like it?" the frog asked as he hopped about.

"Ever so much!" said Thumbelina. "I'm having a wonderful time!"

Do you think it would be fun to be tiny? What would you want to do if you were as small as Thumbelina?

Suddenly… *splash!* The frog dove under the water and Thumbelina sank underwater with him.

"Glug! Glug! Glug!"

The tiny girl popped back to the surface. The frog stared at her in surprise.

"Don't you like the water?" he asked.

"Glug! Glug! Glug!" Thumbelina gasped. "I do. But I cannot play under it like you do. After all, I'm not a frog."

"Oh, I'm so sorry!" the frog exclaimed. "You were so small that I had forgotten."

Poor Thumbelina was dripping wet.

So the frog took her to Auntie Mouse's house, where she could dry off and have a hot drink.

Thumbelina had never seen such a clean and tidy home.

"Come in, my dear. Sit down by the fire," the mouse said quite kindly.

The hot chocolate was delicious. And hungry Thumbelina ate two whole slices of apple pie.

In the days that followed, Thumbelina made a host of new friends. They were as tiny as she was. Even standing up, they were no taller than a blade of grass, but they all made Thumbelina feel at home.

The painted butterflies even offered to paint red dots on her white dress. "How pretty you look," they said.

"Thank you," said Thumbelina.

 *Do you like the red dots that the butterflies are painting on Thumbelina's dress? What color would you choose if you were painting them? What's your favorite color? Why?*

In addition to the butterflies, Thumbelina met the hedgehog, Grandad Mouse, the cricket, the snail, and many others. They liked Thumbelina, and she liked them.

With their help, she built herself a pretty little cottage in a big tree trunk. Thumbelina felt like she had finally found herself a real home.

During the day, she was as happy as can be.

 *Doesn't Thumbelina look happy? What are your favorite things to do during the day?*

But when night fell, Thumbelina grew afraid. She often had bad dreams and woke up trembling.

One night, when she had awakened many times, she went outside. The sky was full of sparkling stars. Thumbelina looked up at them.

Suddenly, she began to call, "I want a star! I want a star! I'm frightened of the dark, and I want a star of my very own!"

From his tree, the old owl hooted. "Nobody is allowed to have stars," he puffed.

Thumbelina burst into tears.

"But I want one!" she cried, her voice full of sadness. "I want a star of my very own!"

The meadow folk, awakened by her sobbing, ran to comfort the tiny girl.

"I have bad dreams at night," Thumbelina explained. "I want a star beside me when I sleep!"

Thumbelina's friends want to help her feel better. Have you ever comforted a sad or scared friend? What did you do?

Thumbelina wandered off to the pond, crying bitterly. By now, she was surrounded by her friends. Auntie Mouse went off to make her a nice cup of chamomile tea. The ladybug offered Thumbelina a large strawberry she had been keeping for a snack.

Then, the cheerful frog—Thumbelina's first friend—arrived. But even he could not help her stop crying.

Poor Thumbelina!

Thumbelina, her eyes brimming with tears, kept staring up at the night sky, sparkling with stars.

"There!" she cried. "I want that one! Look—it's bigger than all the others!"

The tiny girl stretched out her arms. "Please, pretty little star, do come down to me!"

And as though by magic, the twinkling star came closer and closer!

Finally, the star landed at Thumbelina's feet.

But it wasn't a star at all! It was an odd little fellow in tails and a top hat.

With a sweep of his hat, he introduced himself.

"I am not a star," he said. "I am a firefly. But I'll be glad to help, if there's anything I can do."

Thumbelina had never seen a firefly before. "Would you like to stay here with me?" she asked, wide-eyed.

"Of course," replied the firefly. "During the day, I must sleep. But I will come to you every night."

And that's what the firefly did.

Each night, he came to Thumbelina's cottage.

Each night, before she went to sleep, he read her
a story.

Each night, he acted as Thumbelina's night light.

And with the firefly close by, Thumbelina was never
afraid of the dark again.

THUMBELINA AND THE FAIRY

One fine spring day, Thumbelina sat on a stone in a meadow filled with clover. She was enjoying the warm sunshine.

All around her, bees buzzed, going from flower to flower.

Suddenly, something dropped out of the sky.

It was a slender gold wand with a glowing tip.

What a lovely wand! Thumbelina picked it up. She looked up into the clear blue sky. But there was nothing there but a little cloud.

"I wonder where it came from," she thought.

She pointed the wand at the petals of a white daisy. And… the petals turned blue!

In fact, Thumbelina discovered that every time she pointed the wand at a flower, it changed color!

Soon, there were pink, blue, and yellow daisies everywhere.

Thumbelina ran to another part of the meadow, full of lilies-of-the-valley and bluebells.

"Wouldn't it be nice," Thumbelina thought, "if these flowers could ring like bells?"

She pointed the magic wand at a bluebell. And a tinkling note floated out of the flower.

She pointed her wand at another. Another sweet note was heard.

 *If you had a magic wand of your own, what would you do with it?*

A butterfly friend of Thumbelina's heard the music and stopped to listen.

"Aren't you clever, Thumbelina!" she said. "Only you could make the flowers play music!"

"I can make the flowers do anything!" Thumbelina boasted. "I can make them change colors. I can make them sound beautiful!"

"Could you make them smell good, too?" the butterfly asked.

"Maybe," Thumbelina said. "Why?"

"Spring is late this year," the butterfly explained. "The violets don't have their scents yet. Maybe you could help!"

"Of course I can," Thumbelina said. And she waved the wand once more.

Then she put down the wand and stood on tiptoe to sniff the nearest violet. "Mmm," she said. "It smells lovely."

A little while later, Thumbelina heard a polite voice from above her head. It was the voice of a lovely fairy with beautiful wings.

"Excuse me," the fairy said. "Did you by any chance see a golden wand? I've lost it in one of these flowery meadows."

Thumbelina quickly shook her head.

"No, no!" she said. "I haven't seen it. I haven't seen it at all."

The poor fairy has lost her wand.
If you had found it, what would you do?
What do you think Thumbelina will do?

The fairy was very sad.

"Oh dear, oh dear," she said. "When the fairy queen finds out that I've lost my wand, she'll take my wings away. I'll never be able to leave the enchanted castle again!"

Tears slowly dripped down the fairy's cheeks.

Thumbelina stood there, the wand behind her back. She didn't want to give the wand back to the fairy! She wanted to keep it. She wanted to become queen of the flowers. She wanted to tell them when to bloom, what color to be… and for that, she needed the wand.

But the poor fairy! It was her wand! What was Thumbelina to do?

Thumbelina held the wand out to the fairy.

"Here," she said, swallowing a lump in her throat. "Here's your wand."

The fairy could hardly believe it.

"Oh, thank you!" she said. "Now I can go back to the fairy queen without being punished. What can I do to repay you? What would you like?"

But Thumbelina, who really wanted the wand back, didn't know what to say.

"I know," said the fairy. She touched a piece of clover with her wand and gave it to Thumbelina.

"Take this magic clover," she said. "Every time you pull off a petal, one of your wishes will come true."

"Oh, thank you!" Thumbelina exclaimed.

The fairy floated up into the air.

"Come back soon and we can play!" Thumbelina called after her.

"I will!" said the fairy as she flew away. "Good-bye!"

Thumbelina looked at the magic clover and wished the first thing she could think of. "I wish...I wish... that I could grow big, like my parents!"

She picked off the first petal and... the magic worked! To her astonishment, Thumbelina found herself enormous! She had giant feet that could crush anything in their path!

Her little friends ran for cover.

"How horrid the world is when you're very big," Thumbelina thought, "and you can't see the tiny, marvelous things that live in the grass beneath your feet."

Thumbelina quickly made another wish, picked off the second petal of the pink clover, and...

> *What do you think Thumbelina's second wish was? If you had a magic clover, what would you wish for?*

...she was back to normal again.

Her little friends rushed joyously to hug her. "What a fright you gave us with those giant feet," said Auntie Mouse. "You nearly squashed poor Frog!"

"Is it safe now?" the frog asked, peaking out from between some blades of grass.

"Oh, yes!" said Thumbelina.

Thumbelina had one wish left.

Everyone had an idea for the wish.

The squirrel wanted to wish for a heap of hazelnuts. The sparrow wanted to wish for a bag of grain. Auntie Mouse wanted to wish for a wheel of cheese.

Thumbelina thought and thought.

Finally, she asked her friends, "What is the most beautiful thing you've ever seen?"

"The rainbow," the butterfly said.

"Yes, yes," chorused the others. "The rainbow is the most beautiful sight in the world!"

"Then I know what I will wish for," said Thumbelina.

> *Thumbelina had only one wish left.*
> *What do you think Thumbelina wished for?*

Thumbelina picked the last petal off the clover and made her wish.

A glorious rainbow appeared in the sky.

Everyone ran to see it. But Puffi, the newest bunny, couldn't keep up with the others.

Thumbelina picked him up gently.

"Come along," she told Puffi. "Let's go see what I wished for. Let's go see the rainbow."

And they did.

THUMBELINA AND THE BUTTERFLY

It was a lovely day in May, and Thumbelina and her little friends were happily playing leapfrog in the meadow.

Everyone was having a wonderful time. Of course, they were very careful of the hedgehog, for his prickles were terribly tickly!

"Oh, Frog!" laughed Thumbelina. "You and Grasshopper are sure to win! After all, you're the best hoppers in the forest!"

Suddenly, an enormous dark shadow covered the sun.
A pair of great wings beat over their heads.

Thumbelina and her friends rushed to hide in the
tall grass.

It was the Black Butterfly! And everyone knew that
when the Black Butterfly was around, no one in the
meadow was safe.

In fact, the very next day, the Queen Bee came to Thumbelina to complain.

"The Black Butterfly has eaten up every drop of the bees' honey!" she said. "And even worse, he wrecked the hive looking for more! What are we to do?"

Thumbelina offered to give the Queen Bee some of her own honey. The Queen Bee thanked her.

"You are generous, Thumbelina," said the Queen Bee. "But there isn't enough honey left in all the meadow to feed my subjects. I fear some of us will starve."

The bees had barely gone when three of Thumbelina's butterfly friends arrived, crying bitterly.

"Oh, Thumbelina," they said. "All our poor flowers are dying! The Black Butterfly has landed on them and smashed their stems!"

Thumbelina came with them to see. And all that the butterflies had said was true! The flowers lay crushed and broken on the ground.

That evening, a meeting was held around the fire. Everyone came, including the King Frog.

"Something must be done!" declared the Queen Bee. "This dreadful monster who steals our honey must be driven away!"

"He has hurt our flowers," a butterfly added. "He might hurt us all!"

Thumbelina, who had been listening quietly, suddenly had an idea.

"I know what we can do," she said.

Have you ever come up with a good idea to help solve a problem? What was it?

The next day, the tiny girl went to a large old pine tree in the woods to look for the sticky stuff that pine trees make, called resin. But none was to be found.

Thumbelina needed the tree resin for her plan to work. So in a loud voice, she spoke to the pine tree.

"Would you like to hear a story?" she asked the old tree.

"Yes," the pine tree replied. "Tell me."

"Once upon a time," Thumbelina began, "there was a little pine tree. It grew beside its mother. But it never got any taller because it didn't get enough sunlight.

" 'You big trees take it all!' the little tree said.

"The mother pine was so sad to see her son so small that she wept and wept until she died of a broken heart," Thumbelina went on. "This left room for the young pine to grow straight and tall."

When the old tree had heard this story, he was so sad that he began to cry.

Quickly, Thumbelina filled a pail with the tree's resin tears.

That night, she tiptoed to where the Black Butterfly was sleeping.

As silently as she could, she dropped the golden resin on the wings of the butterfly.

Then, she hid in the thick grass and waited for the monster to awaken.

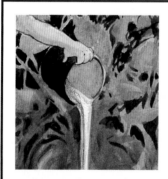

Why do you think Thumbelina dripped resin on the Black Butterfly's wings? What do you think the resin will do?

The next day, when the sun was high in the sky, the Black Butterfly awoke, stretched himself, and spread his wings to fly.

But he soon found flying difficult. His wings were very sticky, and every time he flapped them, the resin made them stick together even more.

At last, the Black Butterfly's wings stuck together for good. He could no longer fly and he fell from the sky. And that was the end of the Black Butterfly.

From their place in the reeds where they were hiding, Thumbelina and her frog friends watched the wicked Black Butterfly fall.

They all cheered. The Black Butterfly would never hurt anyone in the meadow ever again.

The Frog King proclaimed Thumbelina the Princess of the Frogs.

The Queen Bee then invited everyone to a great party. For days on end, the bees buzzed busily from flower to flower until dozens of jars had been filled with honey for the guests.

Thumbelina, Auntie Mouse, the butterflies and bugs and bees, the sparrow, and the hedgehog danced and sang and had a wonderful time!

And Thumbelina did not forget the old pine tree. He could not come to the party, so the tiny girl went to him. She gave him a big hug.

"If it weren't for you, kind tree," she told him, "the Black Butterfly would still be stealing the bees' honey and hurting the flowers. Thank you for the gift of your sticky resin tears."

"You're welcome," said the pine tree. He smiled happily. He was happy he could help Thumbelina and her friends.

THUMBELINA AND THE SURPRISE VISITOR

During the winter, snows fall on the meadow. So Thumbelina and her friends stay at home when the sun goes down, cozy and comfortable.

The lights in their homes shine brightly here and there in the wood. And woodland creatures are always welcome to visit and warm themselves around the fire.

One morning, Thumbelina's little friends were playing in the snow.

A mouse was bringing home an ear of corn for a mouse supper.

The bunnies were building a giant snowrabbit. What fun they were having!

Auntie Mouse was going to visit the Princess of the Frogs.

And who could that be?

Who is the Frog Princess?

Do you remember?

It was Thumbelina, of course! The Frog King had named her the Princess after she saved the forest from the Black Butterfly.

Auntie Mouse had promised to come and help Thumbelina do her daily baking. And she was as good as her word.

Squirrel was there, too, cracking the hazelnuts. Another little mouse tended the fire.

Thumbelina rolled out some dough for a pie. Mmmm! Hazelnut pie! It was the squirrel's favorite!

After the baking was done for the day, Thumbelina was tired. So she and her friends went to bed. Auntie Mouse, the little mouse, and the squirrel stayed the night, since it was too late for them to get home safely.

Thumbelina slept soundly, the way you do when you've done a good day's work.

But as she slept, two enormous yellow eyes stared at her from outside the window! Whose eyes could they be?

Thumbelina was awakened by a scratching sound from outside her cottage.

She jumped up and ran to the door. Her friends heard her and got up, too.

"What's wrong?" asked Auntie Mouse.

"I heard something outside," Thumbelina said.

She opened the door and shone her lantern into the dark, snowy meadow.

But there was nothing there.

"Perhaps you dreamed it," the little mouse said.

"Perhaps," said Thumbelina. And they all went back to sleep.

> *Dreams can sometimes seem real! Have you ever had a strange dream?*

But Thumbelina hadn't dreamed it.

The next day, the bunnies discovered that someone… or something… had been standing outside of Thumbelina's window. There were fresh tracks in the snow.

The tracks were very strange indeed. No one had ever seen tracks like these before.

Were they footprints… or something else? Who could have made them? Nobody knew.

But Thumbelina wasn't taking any chances.

That evening, she decided to bar her doors and windows with planks of wood.

The bunnies cut the wood to the right size. The squirrel hammered the wooden planks over the windows. Thumbelina propped a big wooden plank against the door.

"We will all be safe in here," Thumbelina told her frightened friends. "Whatever is outside will not get in."

Far, far away, a little old man lived in a cave lit by a huge fire that never went out.

The little old man was a blacksmith. Night and day, day and night, he hammered at his forge, while a mole used bellows to blow air on the fire and keep it hot. An otter cared for his tools and made the little old man's supper.

The little old man was very, very old. Even the otter and the mole didn't know how old he was. And all his life, he had worked at his forge. He was very good at what he did.

And tonight, he was making something very special.

 *Do you know what a forge is? What do blacksmiths make?*

Early the next morning, just as a pale sun had risen, the otter set out from the forge with the little old man on his back. Behind the little old man was a mysterious bag full of mysterious boxes. Behind the bag sat the mole.

"How long will it take to get there?" the little old man asked the otter.

"It took me most of a day the last time," the otter said. "And with you and the mole on my back, it will take a little longer. But we will be there before nightfall."

That evening, Thumbelina and her friends barred the door once again.

Whatever it was that had made the tracks could not possibly get into her house.

But suddenly, she heard a scraping and scratching at the door. Then, someone knocked loudly.

Thumbelina and her friends were very frightened.

Who could it be?

Who do you think it is? If you were there with Thumbelina, what would you do?

Suddenly, Thumbelina's little house began to shake and shiver.

And Thumbelina and her friends heard a strange sound indeed.

It was coming from under the floor!

The sound got louder and louder.

Then—oh, my!—the floor rose up. A pink nose poked into Thumbelina's kitchen.

What could it be?

It was a mole. And he was smiling!

"I'm so sorry to enter your house this way," he told the surprised Thumbelina. "But no one answered my knock at the door. And we have something very important for you…"

That's when Thumbelina and her friends found out what was in the boxes that the little old man carried.

They were presents for Thumbelina—lovely things the little old man had made especially for her at his forge! And there were presents for her friends, too—carrots for the bunnies, hazelnuts for the squirrel, and a new pincushion full of lovely pins for Auntie Mouse.

"Even where I live, the forest sings your praises, Thumbelina!" said the little old man. "These gifts are for you and your friends, to thank you for the good things that you do."

Thumbelina clapped her hands. "And to think I was frightened of you!" she laughed. "Thank you. Can you stay for supper? I baked a cake the other day."

"Don't mind if I do," said the little old man. And he had two whole slices of Thumbelina's cake before he headed home.

It was very, very good.

THE SISTERS IN THE LITTLE HOUSE

Once upon a time, in a lovely little house in an especially beautiful meadow, there lived six sisters. They loved each other very much, even though they were all quite different.

The girls' mother had died many years before and their father's work often kept him away from home. As the oldest, Jennifer took care of her sisters when their father was away working.

One lovely spring day the sisters were planning to have a picnic in the meadow. Jennifer was picking flowers for their table. As she gathered flowers, Kitty the cat played in her basket, doing her best to catch a golden bee.

Betty, the youngest of the sisters, helped Jennifer bring the table and chairs outside for the picnic. Though Betty was the smallest in the family, she tried hard to be helpful.

"I hope Dinah and Sara remember the strawberries," Betty said.

"I'm sure they will," Jennifer answered. "There! These flowers look lovely."

In fact, the whole world looked lovely on this perfect spring day.

> *What's your favorite season? What do you like about it?*

Jennifer and Betty went into the little house to finish making the treats for their picnic.

Jennifer tasted some icing for the cake as Kitty rubbed against her legs.

"Not quite enough sugar," Jennifer decided.

Betty was beating the whipped cream and looked up when she heard a noise outside the window.

"There are Dinah and Sara now," she said. "And I don't see the strawberries anywhere!"

"Don't worry, Betty," said Jennifer. "If they've forgotten, they'll simply go back to the woods and get some."

As it turned out, Sara and Dinah *had* forgotten the strawberries!

"We'll go pick them right now!" Dinah promised.

"I know where the best strawberries can be found!" Sara added.

Dinah was the tomboy of the family, always on the move, never still for a moment. Sara was the bookworm and very clever. She often helped the others with their homework.

By the time Dinah and Sara had returned, the picnic was in full swing.

Anna was there, of course. She was the next to oldest after Jennifer. She was very pretty, with long golden hair and pink cheeks. She was also very kind and was always giving her hair ribbons away to the other girls.

Sally, with her brown hair in ringlets, munched on a cookie. Sally could draw beautiful pictures, recite poetry, and play the flute. She could also act so well that

when she played a sad heroine, she made all the girls cry—though no one was crying today. It was too beautiful, and the food was too good!

And you've already met Jennifer. She was everyone's best friend, the one they turned to when they needed help.

Even the family pets joined them for the picnic that day.

Kitty lapped at her little bowl of milk.

Zero the dog had his own seat, complete with cup and saucer.

And the girls all had a wonderful time.

> *Jennifer and her sisters are all different.*
> *Which one of the girls are you most like?*

After the girls had eaten all they wanted to eat, it was time to play.

Betty took out her ball, and she and Zero played catch while Kitty watched.

Then the girls linked hands and danced around the meadow, laughing and singing their special song.

This is what they sang:

"We've got seven special treats,
Jellies, lemonade, and sweets,
Cakes and cookies are our dream,
Candy and chocolate ice cream."

As they danced, Anna's hat blew away in the wind, looking like a giant butterfly.

After they were done, Dinah had an idea.

"Let's go up to the attic and play dress-up!"
she said.

The children were delighted.

"All right," said Jennifer.

She led the way up the stairs. Behind her,
Dinah and Sara talked about what they
would wear.

Anna was already pretending
to be a great lady.

Behind Anna was Sally.

And behind Sally—oops!—was Betty.

"I'm a lady in waiting!" Betty laughed.
"And I just tripped on Sally's train!"

What kind of train is Betty talking about? Are there other words that sound the same with different meanings?

At the top of the stairs, Jennifer opened the door. The attic was a magical place, full of so many interesting things to look at!

There were trunks full of beautiful old clothes. There were lots of old books for Sara to read. There were toys, an accordion, and a trumpet that Sally grabbed the moment she saw it.

And right in the middle of the floor was a large dress-maker's dummy. It stood there like a fine lady, wearing a huge hat.

Anna draped herself in a cape and waved a pretty fan as she looked at her refection in an old mirror that hung from the ceiling.

"Look at me!" Anna cried happily.

The young ladies all chose clothing from the trunk and made up stories about their outfits.

Anna was already wearing the blue cape, of course.

"I am a great lady on my way to the Duke's ball in the kingdom of the dragonflies," she announced.

Jennifer found a fancy dress to go with the huge, beautiful hat.

Dinah, wearing a bowler hat and carrying a walking stick, gave Jennifer her arm.

Betty, just as promised, was a lady-in-waiting. She held the train of Jennifer's dress. In her other arm was an old doll she had discovered in a corner.

Sara was dressed in a brown cloak and wore a pot on her head. In her hand was a large book. "I am a great teacher!" she proclaimed. "If you need something explained, come to me!"

"Let's go outside!" said Jennifer.

Sally blew on her trumpet. And the others agreed that going outside was a very good idea.

When they reached the meadow, the air was fresh and crisp. What a beautiful day to be outdoors!

Sally went first. The others laughed as they tripped over their long dresses. Zero followed them, pulling on Anna's cape.

"Stop it, Zero!" Anna said.

The meadow sparkled with new spring colors that matched the colors of the girls' dresses. The flowers swayed gently in the spring breeze, nodding greetings to the girls and gossiping with one another. But the girls, of course, knew none of this.

Sally blew on the trumpet as they approached the woods, singing as they went:

"We've got seven special treats,
Jellies, lemonade, and sweets,
Cakes and cookies are our dream,
Candy and chocolate ice cream!"

By the time they finished singing, they had reached the forest.

If you were one of the flowers in the meadow, what would you be talking about?

It was lovely to stroll in the silent woods. The girls walked among the trees till the leaves became so thick that light could hardly sneak through.

The woods smelled of pine trees and moss and strawberries. And the ferns looked like they had been stitched by fairies.

Suddenly, the girls heard something. It was a soft, moaning sound. What could it be?

It was Jennifer who noticed the rabbit.

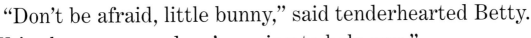

"Look," she whispered. "There's a bunny in the grass." Then she saw something else.

"Oh, no!" she said. "Its paw is caught in a trap. We must rescue it!"

"Don't be afraid, little bunny," said tenderhearted Betty. "We're here now, and we're going to help you."

Working together very carefully, the girls forced open the trap with a thick stick of wood.

"We must take him home and bandage his paw," Jennifer told the others when the rabbit was free.

Jennifer gently picked up the bunny and the girls headed home.

> *What will the little bunny need after the girls take him home? Have you ever helped a wild animal?*

The little house was full of activity that night.

Sara found a book that told the children how to bandage the bunny's paw.

Sally brought hot water and a cloth.

Anna brought the bandages.

And very carefully, Jennifer, with Betty's help, cleaned his paw and did the bandaging.

"This bunny is bigger than all the other wild rabbits," said Sara.

"He must be the king!" Betty gasped.

"Yes," exclaimed the others. "The king of the rabbits!"

"But all the other rabbits live on the hill," Sara said. "What was he doing in the forest?"

"Perhaps he was searching for a place with plenty of food for the other rabbits," Anna suggested. "How brave he is!"

"They must be worried about their king," said Jennifer. "We must do everything we can to help him."

The bunny gazed at Jennifer as if to thank her.

"You'll see," Jennifer told him. "You will soon be back with your friends!"

The rabbit stayed with them for several days until his paw was completely healed. Then it was time to set him free. The girls were sorry to say good-bye to their new friend.

Before going to bed that night, they gathered at the window.

"See how silvery the meadow is," said Jennifer.

Then the children saw an amazing sight!

There stood their very own rabbit, with a host of other rabbits, all gazing up at them.

"It's our friend!" said Jennifer. "He's come to say good-bye!"

"So it is! So it is!" the others cried. "And he *is* the king of the rabbits. He's brought all the other rabbits from the hill."

"It's magic!" Betty said, leaning over the sill for a better look.

"Hello, little bunny! We love you!" the children called.

That night, all six girls had a wonderful dream.

In each dream, the bunny said, "I love you, too!"

Maybe Betty was right, and there was something magical going on that night.

What do you think?

In this story, the girls let the bunny go. Would you have done the same thing? Why?

BETTY AND THE FOREST CREATURES

Jennifer and her sisters lived near a very kind man and his wife. They could always be counted on to help if the girls needed something while their father was away.

The girls wanted to give them a gift to show their thanks. They decided to send them a beautiful basket of apples from their very own apple tree.

Jennifer polished the apples and carefully laid them in a basket.

Each of the girls offered to take the basket to their neighbors' house. But Betty looked so hopeful that Jennifer smiled and said:

"I think it would be best if Betty went."

So Betty happily set out. It was a lovely day. The flowers in the meadow danced gently in the soft breeze.

"They look all dressed up for a ball," Betty thought to herself. "The buttercups are the princes and the daisies are princesses. Aren't they pretty!"

Betty walked and walked. Soon, she grew hungry. The apples looked so delicious that she simply couldn't resist.

"No one will miss one apple," she decided, taking a bite.

Betty soon came to the river. A mother duck and her ducklings swam beside the tall reeds.

"Welcome home, ducks!" Betty said. "Did you have a good winter? How far you must have come! And what a lot of things you must have seen!"

The ducks just quacked.

A tree trunk was floating close to the bank of the river. A little nest was stuck in its branches.

"Oh!" cried gentle Betty. "A nest! Are there any eggs in it? If there are, I will move the nest to a safer place."

Very carefully, Betty climbed onto the tree trunk. But the nest was empty.

"The babies have already flown off on their own adventure," she thought.

While Betty was thinking about the baby birds, the trunk began to shift gently away from the bank.

Suddenly, Betty noticed that she was floating down the river. And she was too far from the bank to return.

At first, it was fun. "I am the Lady of the Mountain, and this is my enchanted boat," Betty pretended.

She floated past the neighbors' house.

"I command you to stop, boat!" she said in her best Lady-of-the-Mountain voice. But of course, the tree trunk just kept on floating.

That was when Betty started to get worried.

The sky was changing color. It would soon be dark. But still the trunk floated along, and now the bank was far, far away.

Suddenly… thunk!

The trunk had landed on the opposite side of the river. And there was no way back in sight.

Betty hopped off the trunk, heaving a sigh of relief.

"At least I'm on dry land," she thought.

Betty looked around. She was standing at the edge of a dark, silent wood.

"Well, I'll simply have to find my way home," she decided. "I think I should go this way…"

She slowly made her way through the trees. Everything was completely silent, and she was all alone.

But the moon was bright overhead, and Betty was a very brave girl.

After walking for awhile, Betty grew tired. She sat down beneath a huge oak tree.

It was getting colder, and Betty shivered. She clutched her shawl tightly around her shoulders.

Suddenly, a little family of hedgehogs padded over and stopped at her feet.

"Hedgehogs!" Betty exclaimed. "How nice! Please, dear hedgehogs, keep me company! I'm a little lost, and I'm all alone."

By this time, Betty was having trouble keeping her eyes open. She decided she might as well go to sleep.

"I'm sure that's what Jennifer would tell me to do," she told herself.

She spread her shawl over a heap of dry leaves at the foot of the tree and used a clump of ferns for a pillow.

Out of the trees came a magnificent deer, with antlers that gleamed like gold in the moonlight. A family of bunnies

came, too, and a badger. They joined the hedgehogs to keep Betty company.

"I must pretend that this is a fairy tale," Betty thought. "I can't wait to tell my sisters all about it. I wonder what they're doing now…"

Can you find all the animals? What other animals might live in a forest?

Back at the little house, Betty's sisters had
started to worry when the sun went down and darkness fell.

"Where can she be?" the girls worried. "Why hasn't she
come home yet?"

"We must go look for her," Jennifer decided.

First they searched the meadow near their house.

"Betty! Betty! Betty!" they called. But there was no answer.

Jennifer waved her lantern to and fro. "Maybe Betty lost her way in the dark," she said.

Sally started to play the trumpet. "She'll hear this if she's not too far away."

The girls kept calling and calling. But Betty did not answer.

Jennifer decided that the girls should follow the path that Betty would have taken to the neighbors' house.

The sisters walked on the path till they reached the river, but there was still no sign of Betty.

Suddenly, Sara noticed something on the ground.

It was the core of an apple.

"Betty came this way!" she exclaimed. "She must have eaten one of the apples."

Then Dinah found some footprints. "These must be Betty's," she declared.

Anna began to cry a little. "I hope Betty hasn't fallen into the water," she sniffed.

"I'm sure she hasn't," said Jennifer. "Maybe she stayed too late at the neighbors and spent the night so she wouldn't have to walk home in the dark. We'll go there in the morning."

Back at the little house, nobody felt like going to bed. Instead, they sat round the table, looking at the apple core Betty had dropped.

They were all very worried about their little sister.

Anna could not help shedding a tear from time to time.

Finally, the long night was over.

Sara saddled the pony and rode to the neighbors' house. A short time later she returned. Betty was not there.

The five girls set out to find her. They went slowly along both sides of the river, shouting Betty's name as loudly as they could. There was still no answer.

Suddenly, Anna stopped.

"That tree trunk over there! With the nest on it!" she cried. "I've seen it before! It used to be near our house! Maybe Betty got onto it and…"

"Yes," Sara nodded. "She could have crossed the river on the tree trunk!"

"If that's what she did, then she can't be far away," Jennifer declared happily.

What clues have the sisters found? Have you ever had to search for clues?

The sisters all gathered on one side of the river and entered the forest. As they walked through the trees, the leaves murmured:

They're searching for the lost child! They've come to find her! To find her! To find heeeerrrrrr...

But the girls, of course, heard nothing of this.

They walked slowly through the woods, calling Betty's name. Suddenly, they stopped in amazement.

There before them stood a beautiful deer with golden antlers. It eyed them steadily, then walked away.

"I think he's trying to help us," Sara whispered.

The girls walked toward the spot where
the deer had stood.

Jennifer and Sarah were the first to see
Betty's umbrella.

And there, under it, was Betty herself.
A blanket of golden leaves covered her,
and three rabbits guarded her as she slept.

Betty opened her eyes. She saw her sisters and smiled. She thought she was dreaming.

Then she sat up. She wasn't dreaming! There were her dear sisters, all around her.

"Betty! We found you! Are you all right?" the girls cried. "Whatever happened to you? We've been searching for you everywhere!"

"Oh, I've been quite all right," Betty told them. "Some forest creatures kept me company. A family of hedgehogs—there they are, behind the tree. And some bunnies. And a beautiful deer—"

"With golden horns!" shouted Dinah. "We saw him, too. He led us to you."

Now, after all the excitement, the girls realized they were very hungry. Jennifer was the first to notice the strawberries growing nearby. So they picked strawberries and had a strawberry and apple feast.

To thank the hedgehogs for helping Betty, the girls invited them back to the little house for a visit. They gave the little animals a bowl of milk as a reward.

"Let's keep them always," said Betty.

Jennifer shook her head. "They're wild animals. They would be unhappy away from the woods. But we can always keep a bowl of milk outside the door. That way, they can come and have some whenever they want!"

And that's exactly what the girls did.

Some animals are wild. They need to be free. But some animals make good pets. Do you have a pet? Would you like one? What kind?

SARA AND THE GOLDEN PUMPKIN

It was a lovely spring day, and the girls were gathered round Sara on the hill behind their little house.

"Winter is over. It's almost time to plant the vegetable garden and the flower beds," she told them. "I've made a list of all the things we need to get ready for planting. Everyone will need to help."

Planting a garden can be lots of fun! Have you ever planted anything? What was it? Did it grow?

First, they needed to buy the seeds. Dinah harnessed the pony to the cart while Sara made a list of what she should buy in the village.

"Get plenty of vegetable seeds," Sara told her. "Broccoli, string beans, carrots, peas… and don't forget the pumpkin seeds!"

While they waited for the weather to get a bit warmer, the girls planted the seeds in little boxes they kept in the barn. It wasn't long before the seeds had all sprouted. They were ready for planting in the ground.

"Just imagine," Betty said. "This little sprout will soon be a big tomato plant."

The next day, Sara supervised the planting of the garden.

"Dinah is very strong, so she'll do the digging," Sara told her sisters.

Dinah jumped to attention. "Yes, ma'am!" she cried.

"Sally will break up the earth with a spade..." Sara went on. "Jennifer will rake the soil, and Anna will plant the seeds. Then Betty will water the plants."

Betty nodded.

Jennifer started to sing. Soon, all the girls were singing, too.

"Off to work, off to work we go!

With trowel and spade and hoe,

A very fine garden we will grow!"

The sisters worked in the garden for the rest of the afternoon. Sara made sure everything was done just right.

All that summer, the girls tended the garden and watched their seedlings growing bigger and bigger.

Anna loved the flowers best of all. Her favorites were the daisies.

Sara and Betty made sure the flowers and vegetables had plenty of water.

Can you name some flowers?
What are some of your favorite flowers?

Weeks passed, and one day the sky grew cloudy and dark. Then it started to rain. It rained as if it would never stop.

The girls sat inside the little house. They watched as the storm raged around them.

"My poor flowers," sighed Anna.

Suddenly, Sara thought of something.

"With all this rain, the river could flood the stable. I'm going to check on the animals and make sure they are all right down there."

Sara raced out to the stable, while her sisters waited.

How do you feel when it rains?

Sara soon came back.

"The animals are very frightened," she told the others. "And the stable is flooding."

"We must move the animals up to the barn," Jennifer decided. "It's on higher ground than the stable. They will be safe and dry there."

The girls put on their rain boots and cloaks and went to help their animal friends.

When the girls got to the stable, the animals were restless. The hen was fluttering about. The lamb was shivering with cold. The rabbit was trembling. The pony was stamping his feet nervously.

"Don't worry," Jennifer told them. "Everything will be all right."

Sara picked up the lamb, who snuggled in her arms. Betty held the rabbit. Anna and Jennifer lifted the hen and her nest of eggs.

"We're taking you to a nice, warm place," Dinah told the little piglet. They carried the smaller animals and led the pony up to the barn.

By the time they fought their way through the storm to reach the barn, the girls were very tired. They decided to stay with the animals that night.

The children lay down on the bags of grain that were stored in the barn. And in spite of the thunder and lightning and rain pounding on the roof, they soon fell sound asleep.

Betty was the first to awaken. The rain had stopped. "The sun is up!" she cried.

The girls rushed to the door, where a wonderful rainbow greeted them.

"I wonder if there is a treasure at the end of the rainbow," Anna said.

"There is a treasure right here!" cried Sara.

For there, next to the hen, were four new baby chicks.

"Cheep, cheep," said the chicks.

It was a beautiful morning. But when the girls went outside, a terrible sight met their eyes.

The flowers had been ruined by the wind and the rain. Their stems were broken and their petals had fallen. And the vegetable plants had been pounded flat by the storm.

"Oh!" Dinah sighed. "And we worked so hard…"

Suddenly, Betty saw something golden at the end of the rainbow. "Could it be a real treasure?" she cried. And she ran over to look. There sat a beautiful golden pumpkin! Since it had survived the terrible storm, Sara knew that it must be a very special pumpkin.

Even though the vegetable garden looked hopeless, Sara quickly took charge.

The children went to work and soon discovered that they could save many of the plants. They rescued many of the flowers, too.

They worked very, very hard. In a few weeks, the garden was thriving again.

They also built a scarecrow to protect the garden from hungry birds. Each day, the garden grew more and more beautiful. And the golden pumpkin grew bigger and bigger.

What vegetables would you like to grow and eat?

Sara herself took special care of the pumpkin.

"It's huge!" said Betty. "The biggest pumpkin in the world!"

"It's the Queen of the Pumpkins," Anna decided.

"Let's enter it in the country fair!" suggested Sara proudly.

"How will we move it?" Dinah asked. "It must be very heavy."

Jennifer turned to Sara. "Sara, is there something in your books that can help us?"

"I'm sure there is," Sara said.

While Sara was looking in her books for something about moving pumpkins, Sally made up a song about the pumpkin:

> *"I'm the giant pumpkin, / I'm as big as big can be,*
> *I grew in storm and rain, / And now I'm something to see!*
> *The rainbow made me shine / As golden as the sun.*
> *I'm as big as I can grow. / Now my garden days are done!"*

Finally, Sara found a way to move the pumpkin.

The girls rolled the pumpkin onto a board and used another piece of wood to lift the pumpkin up.

They put round logs under the board and rolled the pumpkin into the pony cart, and Sara drove it to the fair.

The excited girls followed on foot.

At the fair, prizes were given out for the biggest and best vegetables.

And Sara's giant pumpkin won first prize!

The girls were very proud of the pumpkin "treasure" that had grown at the end of their rainbow. They cheered and cheered.

And then they made lots of pumpkin pies!

DINAH AND THE RESCUE

It had been snowing for three days, and the little house was covered with snow.

It was very beautiful outside, but it was cold.

Inside, it was warm and cozy.

Sally was peeling chestnuts while Dinah stood in front of the fire, roasting them. They smelled delicious.

Sara was mixing batter for a cake.

Anna was doing the mending.

Betty played a song on the accordion. Her music made the work go faster.

And Jennifer was setting the table
   for supper.

After dinner, the sisters went upstairs to their cozy beds.
Anna was the first to drop off to sleep.
"Surprise!" Sally giggled as she tossed a pillow at Sara.
Betty looked for her missing teddy bear (who was sitting
right on her pillow).
Jennifer brushed out her hair. Kitty lay at the foot of her
bed, sleeping soundly.

Dinah wasn't sleepy at all. She stared out at the evening sky. White flakes of snow drifted down.

As she watched, the snow stopped.

"If it doesn't snow any more, I can go skating in the morning!" she thought, smiling.

She could not have known that outside their little house, a wild dog was looking for food. He was tired and very hungry.

The next morning, Dinah was the first to awaken. She was so excited about going skating that she didn't wait for the others to wake.

She dressed quietly. Then she packed her breakfast, took her skates, and went outside.

The pond was near the house. In the winter, it froze over. It was perfectly safe except for one patch where the ice was thin. The girls made sure never to skate near it.

Dinah left her breakfast on the ground nearby. She strapped on her skates and stepped out onto the pond. The snow was silvery on the trees. A beaver watched her glide on the ice.

She never saw the dog. But he smelled her breakfast! Dinah had packed sausages, and the poor dog was so hungry he couldn't resist.

Suddenly, Dinah noticed him, sniffing at her basket. Because she was watching the dog, she wasn't paying attention to where she was skating. Before she knew it, she was on the thin patch of ice!

The ice cracked. And Dinah fell into the icy water.

"Help! Help!" she cried.

She looked up. And there, not six inches from her head, was the wild dog!

She saw his sharp, white teeth and gleaming eyes.

And then… the dog grabbed her jacket, and Dinah felt herself being pulled gently from the water.

She was safe! The dog had rescued her!

Dinah was wet and cold. She knew she had to hurry home to get warm and dry.

So she started to run back to the little house. The dog ran with her, as if to protect her from harm.

From the house, Anna saw Dinah running through the snow, and quickly raised the alarm. The dark shadow plunging along behind her might be a dangerous wolf!

"Quick! Quick! Dinah's in danger!" Anna cried.

However, the girls soon found Anna was mistaken.

"He saved my life!" Dinah told them, shivering.

The girls put Dinah to bed with a hot water bottle and a cup of tea. Jennifer insisted on taking her temperature. The dog waited patiently outside.

Then the girls turned their attention to him. At first, he was too shy to come inside the house. But Jennifer put a bowl of warm milk with bits of bread in it down on the floor.

Soon, the dog began to eat. He ate and he ate.

"The poor thing is starving!" Jennifer said.

"He's very thin," Sara added.

Later that day, all the girls went outside to play in the snow. Even Dinah came.

"I'm feeling much better," Dinah said. "Thanks to you," she told the dog, hugging him.

The dog wagged his tail.

"I think I'll call you Hero," Dinah decided.

Hero wagged his tail again and licked Dinah's face. He was very happy to have found a home. And he was even happier to have found Dinah.

It had been a wonderful, rescue-full day!

SALLY AND THE PORTRAIT

The days passed happily for the six young ladies in the little house. One day, Dinah came home from the village holding a large poster.

"Look, everyone!" she called. "There is going to be an auction in town. All the money will go to charity. We should help by giving them some things that they can sell."

All the girls decided right away what they would make for the auction—except for Sara. "What can I make that someone would want to buy?" she asked herself, as she walked through the fields.

Sara looked around at the beautiful flowers and plants. Then she had an idea.

"I'll make a book!" she decided. "A book about plants and flowers. I'll draw the pictures and label each one!"

Sara started painting her book right away.
She worked very hard. She hoped that her book would
fetch a lot of money at the auction!

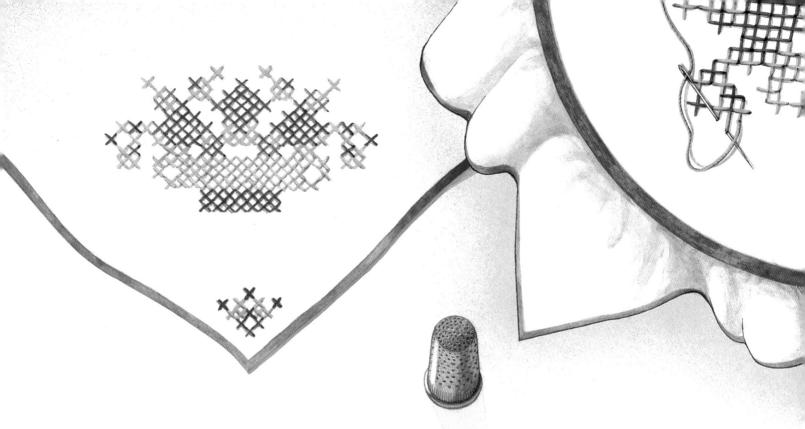

In the meantime, Anna was doing embroidery.
She was very good at it.

The only problem was, Kitty loved to play with her balls
of yarn. Kitty kept getting all tangled up!

*What would
you like to
make or draw
for an auction?*

Jennifer decided she would decorate a vase and donate it to the auction.

She used blue paint to make a picture of the little house on the vase.

"I hope that the new owner will enjoy this as much as I have liked making it," she thought.

Betty was making a necklace out of beads when Kitty knocked all the beads to the ground.

"Oh, oh, dear me," Betty cried.

She crawled under the table, picking up beads. "I'll never find them all," she sighed.

But she did. And soon she finished the necklace. It turned out very well indeed.

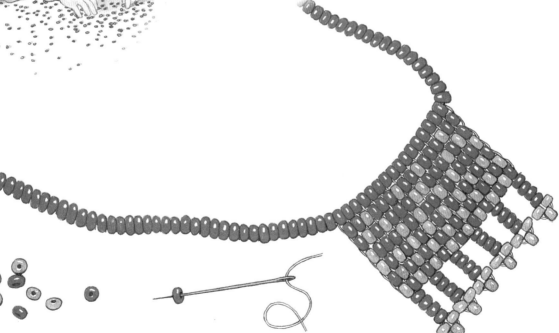

Dinah was just coming back to the house with the materials for her project. She had decided to weave a basket and then decorate it. Baskets are useful, and Dinah thought that it would fetch a good price.

After the basket was woven, Dinah painted large, colorful flowers all over it.

Sally was also painting something, a self-portrait—a picture of herself.

She began by setting up her easel next to a mirror.

But no matter how hard she tried, she couldn't make the picture look like her. First, she couldn't get her hair right. Then, one eye was bigger than the other.

Sally was so upset that she was about to burst into tears.

Just then she heard a knock on the door.

> *What would you wear if you painted a picture of yourself?*

It was Anna.

And that gave Sally a wonderful idea.

"Anna!" Sally begged. "Could I paint your picture? It will be much easier than painting my own!"

"All right," said Anna.

Sally started to draw Anna on her canvas right away.

Now, before you learn what happened to the portrait Sally painted of Anna, you should know that not far from the little house, there was a winding road that led to an ancient castle. It was in the middle of a beautiful forest. There were foxes in the forest, and many people enjoyed fox hunting there.

One morning, the sound of a horn could be heard through the trees. It was time for another fox hunt.

A nearby fox heard the horn and took off through the forest.

The hunting dogs led the chase, followed by a young man on horseback.

That morning, Anna had left the house early. She was taking Sally's painting to town for the auction. It was a beautiful fall day, and the leaves on the trees had turned warm shades of red and orange. Anna decided to take a shortcut through the woods.

She was surprised to find a young man resting by the base of an old oak tree. Beside him was a white horse, grazing on the grass.

The young man introduced himself — he was Count Edward and lived in the nearby castle. Anna curtsied prettily and told him her name.

"Where are you going with that portrait?" Edward asked.

Anna told him the story of the auction, and how the portrait had come to be painted.

Count Edward stared at the painting for a long time. He was disappointed when Anna said good-bye and went on her way.

When she arrived home, Anna could think of nothing but her meeting with the young horseman.

"Count Edward is very handsome," she told Sally. "He seems to be about our age. And he liked your painting very much."

"I am sure he was not as interested in the painting as he was in you," Sally said, smiling.

That night Sally dreamed that she was a great artist, painting a large picture on a famous building. When she dropped her brush, a handsome prince picked it up.

Anna had a dream, too. It started out badly. A pack of hunting dogs raced through the sky. They were chasing a fox. They tore right through Sally's painting!

But then, from far away, she saw a man on a white horse ride up.

"Hurry, Anna! Jump on, or they will catch us!" he called to her. So she did.

They rode and rode through a sky full of clouds until they reached a castle.

Anna turned and saw that the rider was Count Edward.

He smiled at her.

What kind of dreams do you have at night? Can you remember what you dreamed last night?

And that's when Anna woke up.

"Anna, Anna! It is seven o'clock!" Sally was shaking her.

"I was having such an interesting dream," Anna said. "I don't want to wake up."

"But today is the auction!" Sally reminded her. "And we have to go and see who buys our painting."

Young Count Edward was the first to arrive at the auction house that morning. He had come to deliver a china tea set donated by his mother.

While it was being unpacked, Count Edward looked around. He was looking for something in particular.

Can you guess what Count Edward was looking for?

There were many things for sale. There
was a bicycle, and a violin, and a teapot,
and dolls and hats and jams and jellies.
And of course, there were all the things
that the girls had made.

Count Edward saw a picture sitting on
an easel, covered by a cloth. He quickly
walked over to it and drew the cloth away.
He smiled to himself. It was exactly the
picture he was looking for— a portrait of
a young lady with long blonde hair.

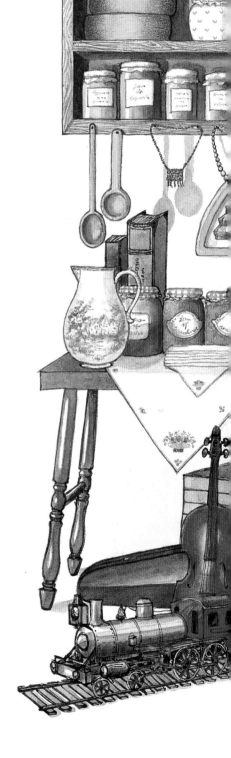

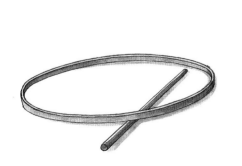

Soon after that it was time for the auction. The auctioneer banged his hammer. "Let the auction begin!" he said in a loud voice.

He auctioned off the bicycle and a flute, a pewter pitcher and the violin. He auctioned off almost everything in the room, including the beautiful things that Sally's sisters had made. Finally, the only things left were the Countess's tea set and Sally's picture.

The tea set sold for a great deal of money. Everyone applauded. After all, the money was going to a good cause.

Finally, it was time to auction off Sally's picture.

But when she took off the cloth… the picture was gone!

A murmur of surprise ran through the crowd.

Sally found a note on the easel. The note read:

"I hereby leave this bag of gold, which I hope will be enough to purchase this beautiful picture."

The note was not signed. Who could have left it? the crowd wondered.

The bag contained more money than anything else had sold for… even the Countess's tea set!

Never had a missing painting been sold for so much money! Sally was very proud.

ANNA AND THE MASKED BALL

A few weeks after the auction, a basket of beautiful flowers arrived at the little house. There were roses and goldenrod, tulips and irises.

And there was a note.

The note and the flowers were from young Count Edward. He had sent them to Anna.

"Dear Anna," the note read. "Please don't mind me calling you by name. After meeting you in the forest, and now that I own a picture of you, I feel like I know you. I hope you and your sisters will come to the castle for the annual Masked Ball. Yours, Edward."

"Hooray! Hooray! We are going to a masked ball!" The young ladies danced around the room.

There was great excitement in the little house after that. What would the sisters wear to the masked ball? They went through all of their clothes and even the boxes in the attic.

Betty tried on a pair of long white gloves. Sally put on a pink bonnet. Sara laced up an old corset. Dinah searched the old trunk.

Jennifer wrapped herself in a beautiful green flowered shawl. And Anna tried on a lacey lavender dress that had belonged to their mother.

"How beautiful!" Jennifer told her.

Anna just blushed.

> *If you were going to a masked ball, what kind of mask would you wear?*

The excitement grew in the days that followed. One by one, each girl decided what to wear to the ball.

There was sewing to be done, and ironing, too, to get their dresses ready. The ball was only two weeks away, and the girls were afraid they wouldn't be ready in time.

Zero the dog couldn't
understand why his young
ladies were staying inside
all the time.

On the other hand, Kitty
the cat was glad for their
company and for the chance
to play with their ribbons
and bows.

Of course, since it was a ball, there would be dancing. The girls practiced as often as they could.

Sara played the piano while Anna twirled.

The girls also found an old gramophone.

"One, two, three, one, two, three," they counted in their heads as they whirled around and pointed their toes.

Gramophones play records—big black plastic disks. Have you ever seen a gramophone or a record? What is your favorite kind of music? Do you like to dance?

"How will we wear our hair?" Betty wanted to know.

The girls spent many hours deciding.

They used combs and hairpins, ribbons and flowers. They put their hair up and they let their hair down. It was fun to experiment.

And of course they would also need masks. For you must remember that this was a masked ball!

Count Edward surprised them by sending a box full of wonderful masks. Some were mysterious, and some were a little scary. And some were sparkly and very beautiful.

"How will we get to the ball?" Dinah wanted to know.
All they had was their little pony cart.

It wasn't very elegant. But the girls soon took care
of that.

They tucked paper roses and bunches of flowers into
the cushions they placed over the bare boards. They
painted the harness with stripes of pink and yellow.
They groomed the pony until his coat shown.

"It still looks like a pony cart," Anna sighed.

"Well," said Jennifer briskly, "it is the best we can do.
And that's that!"

But kind Count Edward had still another surprise in store for Anna and her sisters when the night of the masked ball arrived.

The girls were in their pretty dresses, ready to go to the ball, when they heard the sound of hooves outside the little house.

A magnificent carriage drawn by four white horses appeared. The coachman leaped to the ground.

"Miss Anna and her sisters?" he inquired.

"Yes..." replied Anna faintly.

"Count Edward has sent me to bring you to the castle whenever you are ready."

"We're ready now!" cried Betty. "Let's go!"

The young ladies climbed into the beautiful coach.

"Isn't this wonderful?" asked Dinah, snuggling into the soft cushions.

The coach bounced along the road. The girls chattered happily. Soon they would be at the ball!

Have you ever gone to a fancy event or party? What did you wear? How did you feel when you were on your way?

Suddenly the bumping grew worse. One of the wheels on the coach had begun to wobble.

The horses slowed and the coach came to a halt.

The coachman got out and bent down to see what had happened.

"I have to go to the castle for help," he told the young ladies. "This wheel must be fixed."

To everyone's surprise, Anna spoke up.

"Please stay with my sisters," she told him. "I will go and fetch help."

The coach can't travel on a wobbly wheel. Do you think the sisters will get to the ball?

Meanwhile, at the castle, Count Edward was getting worried.

"Anna and her sisters are late," he told his mother, the Countess. "Something must have happened. I'll go see."

Count Edward rode out into the forest. And there, through the mist, he saw Anna!

She told him what had happened. He swept her up on his horse and rode back for help.

Soon the young ladies were delivered to the ball, just in time for the first dance.

And whom do you think Count Edward chose to be his partner? Anna, of course!

The music started.
Count Edward took her hands.
The whole thing was like a
beautiful dream.

"You must dance all the dances with me tonight,"
Count Edward told Anna.
And she did.